Out on bikes with Grampy

Written by Anna Jarvis
and illustrated by Hannah Asen

Play Together on Pedals

Grampy and I are off out on bikes. We test our bells. Mine's the loudest.

Ping Ping,

Ring-a-ring-a-Riiiiing,

"Ready, steady...

GO!"

I'm really fast.
"Grampy, you can't catch me!"

"Stop at the lines!"
shouts Grampy...
so I do.

Toot Tooot

TOOOOOOOT

On the road, the cars and trucks whizz past.
It makes me wobble... but I stay on.

Grampy stretches out his arm to show them which way we're going. I do too.

The City   Railway Path

Now we're bumping up a steep track.
"This... was once... a railway line... and... steam trains... puffed... up this hill..." puffs Grampy.

My bike sounds like a train.

"WhoooHooooooo!"

Clickety clack, clickety clack

"Here's the old platform. It's higher than the track to help people get onto the trains."

"ALL ABOARD..."

Ping Ping

I look down at Grampy. Grampy looks tiny.
"Careful!" calls Grampy, as I leap off the platform.
"We all need to get home in one piece."

Grampy stares at his map and I stare at mine.

"The turning should have been back there... I didn't see it," mutters Grampy. **"I didn't see it too,"** mutters me.

"Never mind," says Grampy. **"Let's go this way."**

We arrive at the mouth of a dark tunnel.
"Shhhhh," whispers Grampy.
**"If you listen carefully, you might hear the
ghost train whistling."** I listen very carefully...

"WHoooHOOOOOOOOOO!"

whoohoos Grampy.

"Race you to the end of the tunnel!" I shout. And I cycle so fast that no ghost train could ever catch me. Not ever!

The track starts to go down, down, down.
It swishes this way and that. It's really good
fun whizzing round the bends!

Weeeeeeeeeee!

"I'm faster than you!" I shout.
"No, I'm faster than you!" shouts Grampy. Grampy is cheating.

Now Grampy is going so fast he disappears around the corner... then I hear a

"OₒOₒOₒOₒOₒOO".

What is that? Is it the ghost train?

Nope. It's just Grampy! **"MoooOOoove over please cows!"** moos Grampy. **"Careful,"** I laugh, **"we all need to get home in one piece!"**

"Here's the turning!" smiles Grampy. I follow Grampy down a narrow path and then suddenly...

We're at a great big loch. With so many birds we can't feed them all.

Then we go on the swings and Grampy swings higher than me.
I let him win. This time.

On our bikes again, we head back to the road.

"That's not a road, that's a car park!" laughs Grampy.
There's beeping and tooting, but nobody's moving at all.
Except us.

"I bet all these people wish they were out on bikes like we are!" I call to Grampy. **"We sure do!"** laugh all the people, before they start tooting again. Grampy and I laugh and wave. Then it's time to head home to hunt for more bird seed.

"Can we go out on bikes again tomorrow?"
I ask. **"Absolutely,"** says Grampy.
"And maybe we'll spot that ghost train too.

Whoooohooooooo!"